BIG ★ KID POWER

I Sleep in a BIG BED

Maria van Lieshout

chronicle books · san francisco

When I was little I slept a lot . . .

Zzzzzzzz

GURGLE

GURGLE

And I slept anywhere.

At night, I slept in my crib . . .

NO,
BIG KIDS
SLEEP IN A
BIG BED!

When it's time for bed,
I crawl under the covers.
We read a story. Or two.

We give kisses
and hugs.

Then I snuggle with my lovey,
and I go to sleep.

If I wake up at night,
things look a little different.

"This bed is
VERY BIG!"

"Where am I?
Where is my crib?
What if my lovey falls out?"

It can take some time to
   feel **okay** in a big bed.

But if I wake up,
   I pull my lovey close,
cuddle up under the blankets . . .

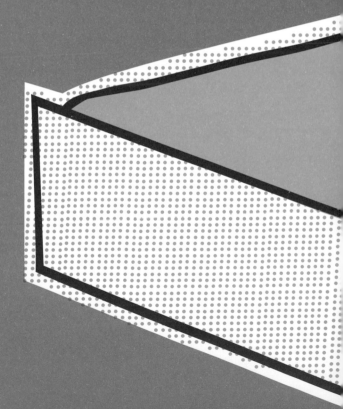

and go back to sleep.

I
LOVE
MY
BIG BED.

I'M A
BIG KID!